FLAT STANLEY

Written by
JEFF BROWN

Illustrated by
Rob Biddulph

EGMONT
We bring stories to life

First edition published in Great Britain 1968.
This edition published in 2019 by Egmont UK Ltd,
The Yellow Building, 1 Nicholas Road, London W11 4AN
www.egmont.co.uk

ISBN 978 1 4052 9155 2

A CIP catalogue record for this book is available from the British Library.

For Barbara and Rod RB

"HEY!"

Arthur Lambchop called
from the bedroom he shared
with his brother Stanley.

Their parents, Mr and Mrs Lambchop,
cared greatly for politeness and correct speech.

"Hay is for horses, not people," said Mrs Lambchop.

"But look!" said Arthur, pointing.

Across Stanley's bed lay his enormous pin board which had fallen on top of him.

Mr and Mrs Lambchop hurried to lift it up. But Stanley wasn't hurt.

"What's going on here?" he said cheerfully.

"Gosh!" said Arthur. "Stanley's flat!"

"As a pancake,"
said Mr
Lambchop.

"Let's all have
breakfast,"
said Mrs
Lambchop.
"Then we can
take Stanley to
see Dr Dan."

Dr Dan examined Stanley.
"How do you feel?" he asked.

"I felt sort of tickly after I got up,"
Stanley said. "But I feel fine now."

"You'll be okay," Dr Dan reassured him.

Mrs Lambchop said she thought that Stanley's clothes would need to be altered to fit him, so the doctor took his measurements.

He was 48 inches tall,

about 12 inches wide,

and half an inch thick.

But Stanley quickly discovered
that being flat could be fun.

In the park, Stanley and Arthur
watched some boys flying kites.

"I would like a big kite," said Arthur.

"You can fly me," said Stanley.

He gave Arthur the spool, attached
the string to his arms and then ran
across the grass to catch the wind.

Up, up, up went Stanley,
soaring high above the trees.

But Arthur got tired
and went off for a hot dog.

He didn't notice when
Stanley became tangled.
Stanley wasn't very
pleased about that!

The next morning, Stanley and Mr Lambchop
bumped into their neighbour, Mr O.J. Dart,
director of The Famous Museum of Art.

Mr Dart looked worried.
"Another valuable painting was stolen
from the museum last night," he told them.
"The thieves work at night by sneakery,
which makes them very difficult to catch!"

But Stanley had an idea . . .

That night in the museum, Mr Dart showed Stanley his disguise. Stanley could hardly speak when he saw it!

But he was a good sport, so he put it on and climbed into an empty picture frame. Mr Dart and the police hid downstairs.

Now Stanley was alone.

Maybe the sneak thieves won't come, he thought. Then . . .

. . . a glow of yellow light shone
suddenly in the centre of the hall.

A trapdoor had
opened in the floor!

The sneak thieves came up into the hall and took the world's most expensive painting off the wall.

"This is it," they laughed. "No one will suspect us!"

Then they spotted Stanley in his frame.

"I thought shepherdesses were supposed to smile," said the first thief. "This one looks fierce!"

Stanley waited until the sneak thieves turned their backs and shouted . . .

WORLD'S MOST EXPENSIVE PAINTING

£999 Billion

"Oh no," whispered the second thief.
"I think I heard the shepherdess yell."

"Talking pictures?" the first thief
whispered back. "We both need a rest."

"You'll get a rest, all right!" shouted Mr Dart, rushing in with lots of policemen. "You'll get ar-rested, that's what!"

The sneak thieves were quickly handcuffed and taken to jail.

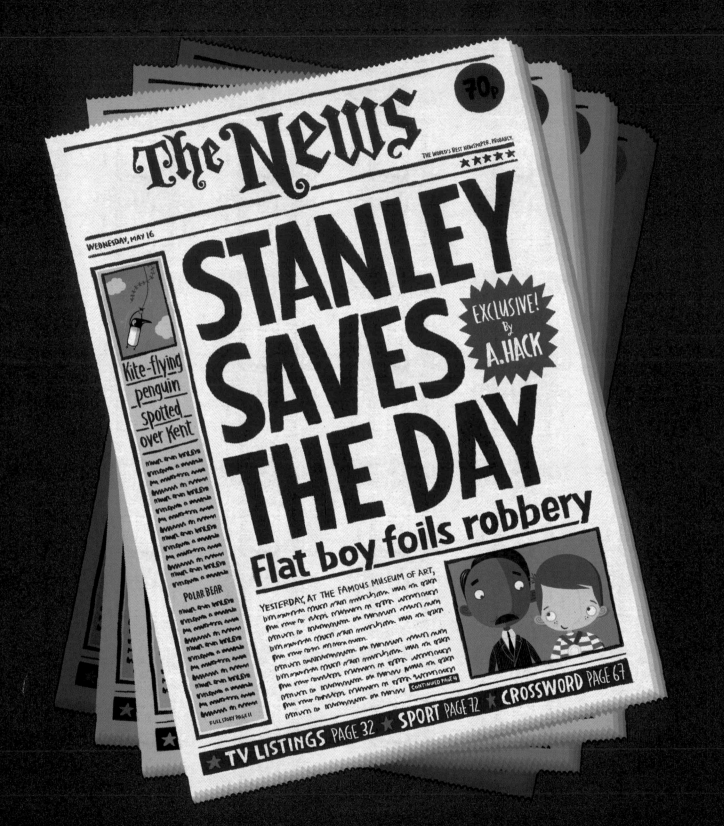

The next day, Stanley got a medal and
his picture was in all of the newspapers.

Stanley was famous. People would point him
out and whisper, "Stanley Lambchop! He's the
one who caught the museum robbers . . ."

But then some mean people
began to make fun of him.
"Hi, Super-skinny!"
they would call.

Later that night, Arthur woke
to the sound of Stanley crying.

"What's wrong?" he said.

Stanley sighed.
"I want to be a regular shape again."

Luckily, Arthur had an idea.

He ran to the big toy box and tossed aside balls, aeroplanes and toy boats.

"Got it!"

he said, holding up an old bicycle pump.

"Okay," Stanley said
after a moment.
"I hope this works."

Arthur began to
pump.

Stanley got BIGGER...

and BIGGER...

and BIGGER.

His pyjama buttons burst off. And there stood
Stanley Lambchop, as if he had never been flat at all.

"Thank you, Arthur," Stanley said. "Thank you very much!"

Mr and Mrs Lambchop
came in to see why the boys
were up so late at night.

"Stanley's round again!"
said Mrs Lambchop.

"I'm the one who did it,"
Arthur said. "I puffed him up."

Mrs Lambchop made
hot chocolate to celebrate
Arthur's cleverness.

Then Mr and Mrs Lambchop
tucked the brothers back into
bed and turned out the light.

"Goodnight," they said.

"Goodnight,"

said Stanley and Arthur.

It had been a long day and very soon
all the Lambchops were asleep.

A light breeze blew through the window . . .

. . . and what do you think happened next?